Don't Do It, Dani!

Collins
RED
STORYBOOK

Don't do it, Dani!

Margaret Ryan

Illustrated by Alan Snow

CollinsChildren'sBooks
An Imprint of HarperCollinsPublishers

First published in Great Britain in Young Lions in 1994
Reprinted by CollinsChildren'sBooks in 1995

3 5 7 9 8 6 4 2

CollinsChildren'sBooks is an imprint of
HarperCollins*Publishers* Ltd.,
77-85 Fulham Palace Road,
Hammersmith, London W6 8JB

Text copyright © Margaret Ryan 1994
Illustrations copyright © Alan Snow 1994

The author and illustrator assert their moral right to be
identified as the author and illustrator of the work.

Printed and bound in Great Britain
by HarperCollins Manufacturing Ltd., Glasgow

ISBN 000 674874 0

Chapter One

If there was one thing Dani Danielson could not resist, it was a dare. If someone dared her to do something – no matter how silly it was – she just had to do it.

At home, her big twin brothers, Roderick and Jamie, dared her to do silly things.

"Dare you to put curry powder in Dad's tomato soup," they said.

Dani knew she shouldn't. She knew

she would get into trouble. But a dare was a dare. So she did.

"EEEARGH COUGH SPLUTTER GURGLE...HELP! WATER, QUICK!...Dani Danielson...just wait till I get my hands on you. I want a word with you. You've put me off tomato soup for life..."

At school, her classmates dared her to do silly things.

"Dare you to jump out on Miss Wheeler in the corridor, and shout BOO!"

Dani knew she shouldn't. She knew she would get into trouble. But a dare was a dare. So she did.

"EEEEEEEK SQUEEEAAAAK...OH MY, WHAT A SHOCK...Dani Danielson...just wait behind at the morning interval. I want a word with you. You gave me the fright of my life..."

And so it went on...and on...and on. A white mouse in her mum's shopping bag. Sticky sweets in her dad's best socks. A hairy spider in Miss Wheeler's lunchtime sandwiches...till finally...

"This dare business has got to stop, Dani," said her mum and dad, "before you get into serious trouble." Then they turned to Roderick and Jamie. "And you two are just as much to blame. Don't dare her to do any more silly things."

"OK," promised the twins.

"This dare business has got to stop, Dani," said Miss Wheeler, "before you get into serious trouble." Then she turned to the rest of the class. "And you lot are just as much to blame. Don't dare her to do any more silly things."

"No, Miss Wheeler," they all promised.

Well, nearly all. One person didn't promise. Morris Clump, youngest and nastiest member of the notorious Clump Gang, didn't promise. He just sat there, chewing his pencil and scowling. He had never forgiven Dani for secretly sticking a notice saying

CLUMP'S A CHUMP on the back of his bomber jacket. He'd gone around school with it on all day, wondering why everyone was laughing at him. He didn't like people laughing at him. He liked people to be afraid of him. So Morris Clump didn't promise. He just sat there, spitting out bits of pencil, and scowling.

Chapter Two

"I really will try hard not to do any more dares," promised Dani when she got home from school that day. "Trouble is, if somebody dares me to do something, something comes over me, and I feel I just have to do it."

"Just don't listen to the people who dare you then," said her mum.

"Stick your fingers in your ears," said her dad.

"Sing at the top of your voice," said

her twin brothers.

"I'll try," said Dani.

But it wasn't easy.

Next morning in class, while Dani was busy working out how many millimetres there were in 6.25 metres, Morris Clump sidled up to her.

"Dare you to do all your sums upside down," he hissed.

"I'm just not listening to you," said Dani.

"DOUBLE dare you to do all your sums upside down in red felt pen," he hissed.

Dani
stuck her
fingers in
her ears.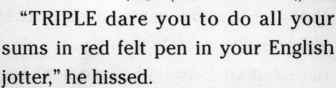

"TRIPLE dare you to do all your sums in red felt pen in your English jotter," he hissed.

"TEN GREEN BOTTLES HANGING ON
THE WALL
TEN GREEN BOTTLES HANGING ON
THE WALL,"

sang Dani at the top of her voice.

"What on earth..?" exclaimed Miss Wheeler. "Dani Danielson, what *are* you doing? Oh, I know. It's another dare, isn't it? Despite all I've said to you, you pay no attention. Well, there'll be extra homework for you tonight, my girl. I meant what I said! This dare business must stop, once and for all."

Dani opened her mouth to protest that the singing wasn't a dare, that she was desperately trying *not* to do a dare, but who would believe her? The class were doubled up with silent laughter, Miss Wheeler was doubly cross with her, and Morris Clump, that double-crossing, cross-eyed toad, was grinning from ear to ear.

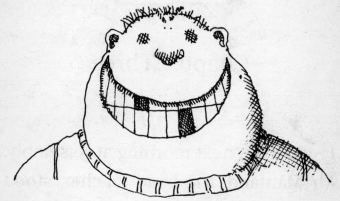

And there was worse to come.

Chapter Three

It came the next morning at Assembly. Mr Maitland, the head teacher, stood up to make a special announcement.

"Greenfield School is going green," he said, laughing at his own little joke. "I have decided that our special project for this term will be WASTE NOT WANT NOT. We are going to set a good example to the rest of the town by recycling our rubbish. No more throwing away our used paper. We shall collect it. No more throwing away our empty cans. We shall collect them. No more throwing away our banana skins. We shall collect them too."

"Think he's finally gone bananas," muttered Dani to her friends Dot and Ben.

Mr Maitland hadn't finished...

"Then, at the end of term, we'll have a Green Fair to show everyone what can be done with rubbish."

"What's wrong with putting it in the bin as usual?" muttered Dani.

"...That way we shall help the environment, and make some money for our local charities as well."

"Oh well, fair enough," thought Dani.

Everybody in the room cheered up immediately. All this collecting business sounded like time off real lessons.

Mr Maitland always announced a special project for each term. Last term Greenfield School had SAVED THE HEDGEHOG. They'd been going to SAVE THE WHALE, but they couldn't be so easily kept in back gardens. The term before that they'd organised a Frog Crossing over a busy stretch of main road. Dani had made up a big poster for that which she'd stuck up by the side of the road. It said:

BEWARE OF THE FROGS

"I wonder what we've to do this term," she muttered. "My mum wasn't too happy with the hedgehog I let sleep in her best hat or the frog spawn the twins dared me to keep in the bath."

"What I need," Mr Maitland was still going on, "is plenty of volunteers. Remember, many hands make light work. Who'll volunteer to collect lots of old newspapers?"

A whole forest of hands went up.

"We get loads of newspapers."

"My dad spends all Sunday reading the sport."

"Hope I don't have to give away my comics."

"Good," beamed Mr Maitland. "Now, who'll volunteer to collect lots of old tins?"

"Me."

"And me."

"And him."

"Good excuse to drink more Coke."

"My mum's home-made soup comes from a tin."

"Hope I get to jump on them."

"That's very good indeed," beamed Mr Maitland. "Now, here's a very special job. Who'll volunteer to set up a compost heap in the playground?"

All went suddenly quiet. There wasn't a sound. Not a voice was heard. Not a hand went up.

"Oh, come along now, boys and girls," encouraged Mr Maitland. There was a muttering and a murmuring...

"Collect smelly old stuff from the rubbish bin? No fear."

"Poke about in soggy tea leaves and eggshells? No way."

"Collect cabbage leaves and horse droppings? No chance."

Then a horribly familiar voice hissed in Dani's ear.

"I dare *you* to volunteer to set up the compost heap, Dani Danielson."

Dani tried not to listen.

"I *double* dare you to volunteer to set up the compost heap, Dani Danielson."

Dani put her fingers in her ears.

"I *triple* dare you to volunteer to set up the compost heap, Dani Danielson."

Dani was just opening her mouth to sing *Ten Green Bottles* when she caught Miss Wheeler's eye. She shut her mouth with a snap.

"Huh, Dani the daring, scared of a dare?" taunted Morris Clump.

Then something came over Dani. A dare was a dare, and she just had to do it. Her hand crept out of her cardigan pocket, slid up past her ear and struggled up into the air.

"I'll volunteer to set up the compost heap, Mr Maitland," she sighed.

"Good girl, Dani," chirruped Mr Maitland, "that's the spirit. Perhaps you might be able to persuade some of your friends to help you."

Dani looked pleadingly at Dot and Ben, but they were already edging away from her, holding their noses, and making POO POO STINKY POO noises.

"Somehow I don't think so," muttered Dani. She turned round and glared at Morris Clump, who just sat there and smiled. In triumph.

Chapter Four

On his way out of assembly, Mr Maitland handed Dani a piece of paper. "This will help you get your compost heap started, Dani," he said. "Just let me know if you need any help. I'm sure I can rely on you to make a good job of it."

Dani nodded and stuffed the piece of paper into her pocket. She put off reading it till the morning interval, then she fished it out and had a look.

It said,

COMPOST HEAP INSTRUCTIONS

1. FIND AN AREA BY THE SCHOOL WALL THAT IS
   FAIRLY SHADY AND NOT TOO DAMP.

"May as well get on with it, I suppose," muttered Dani, and went to look.

She found the ideal place , but some boys were playing football there.

"Hi, Dani. Want a game?"

"No, thanks. This is where the school compost heap's to be. Want to help organise it?"

"Yuk," they all said and moved off.

Dani looked at the paper again.

2. FIND SOME OLD BRICKS TO SUPPORT THE
   COMPOST HEAP AND LET THE AIR
   FLOW THROUGH.

"Bricks," muttered Dani. "Now where am I supposed to find bricks? I know, I'll ask Mr Merridew."

Mr Merridew, the school caretaker, was enjoying his morning coffee when Dani found him in his little room.

"Morning, Mr Merridew. I'm in charge of setting up the school compost heap for this term's special project, WASTE NOT, WANT NOT. Have you got any bricks you could give me?"

"No."

Dani looked at a neat pile of bricks on the floor at the caretaker's feet.

"What's that?"

"That's not bricks. That's my coffee

table. Uses it to put my cup on, see, whenever I can get a minute's peace from you lot."

Dani thought for a moment. "If you could just *lend* me the bricks... er... em... coffee table for a while, I could let you have some good compost for your garden."

Mr Merridew thought for a moment. "Oh, all right. Go on, then."

Dani carted the bricks, two at a time, over to the site she had chosen, and set them out neatly.

Then she read the third instruction.

3. ASK YOUR CLASS TO BRING IN SOFT WASTE.

THINGS LIKE ORANGE PEEL, CABBAGE LEAVES,

ONION SKINS, STINGING NETTLES,

AND ANIMAL MANURE.

Dani laughed out loud when she read this. "I'm saved," she cried. "My class can hardly remember to bring in their PE kit on the right day, never mind these awful things. I can forget about setting up this compost heap. It'll never get off the ground."

Chapter Five

But she was wrong. Mr Maitland had sent letters home to all the parents asking for their help, and the next morning in the playground, at the site of the compost heap, Dani was bombarded with piles of polythene bags. They contained some very interesting things.

"We had to have cabbage last night so you could have the thick green outer leaves."

"My mum sent you all our eggshells."

"My dad's always having cups of tea, so he saved you all his soggy tea bags."

Then, just before the bell rang, a heavy, fat polythene bag came flying over the school wall, and landed right at Dani's feet. It burst open, and its contents spilled out.

"YEUCH," yelled Dani. "Horse droppings."

Everyone but Dani scattered, holding their noses. Then a smirking Morris Clump came swaggering through the school gates. "Did you like the little present I sent you, Dani

Danielson? Picked it up as I crossed the fields this morning. It's nice and fresh, you know. Probably still warm. I just knew you'd be pleased with it."

Dani didn't reply, just pulled on the rubber gloves she had brought from home, and began piling everything onto her heap.

"If this doesn't cure me of doing dares," she muttered. "Nothing will."

That afternoon, Mr Maitland came round the classes, and announced that the special project had begun well.

"The newspapers and cans are beginning to pile up, and I notice that the compost heap has got off to a good start too. Keep bringing in the waste materials, and Greenfield School's Green Fair will be a great success. As an extra bonus, there will be a special prize for the class that

works the hardest."

Everyone brightened up. Last term's special prize had been chocolate sundaes.

"Right," said Dani to Dot and Ben,

"if I must do that awful compost heap, then at least it's a start towards that prize for our class. It would be great if we won. I've got a library book* that's got lots of good recycling ideas in it. I'll tell the others all about it later."

Dani got her chance when, just before lunchtime, Miss Wheeler was called out of the room. Dani leapt up onto her desk.

"Pay attention, everyone," she said, in a stern voice not unlike Miss Wheeler's. "Which is the best class in Greenfield School?"

"Ours."

"Which class will do best at the Green Fair?"

"Ours."

"Which class will win the special prize?"

"Ours."

"Correct on all three," grinned Dani, "and here's how we'll do it. Dot, you organise a group to make collage pictures from scrap materials to decorate the school hall. 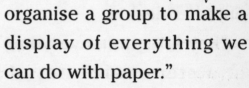 Ben, you organise a group to paint cardboard boxes as toy boxes. Emma, you organise a group to make a display of everything we can do with paper."

And on and on she went...

"Great ideas, Dani. We're bound to win the special prize," said everyone.

Well, not quite everyone. Morris Clump didn't think much of the special prize or the great ideas.

"So that's what you're up to, Dani Danielson," he muttered. "Hoping that if our class wins the special prize you'll get some of the credit. Well, you can hope all you like, but it'll do you no good. Big brothers, Boris and Norris, and I are working on a little plan that will land you in some really serious trouble. I'll teach you to try to make a fool of Morris Clump."

And he smiled. Evilly.

Spring Clean Your Planet by Ralph Levinson
(Beaver Books)

Chapter Six

Dani set to work to prepare for the Green Fair. First she went round all the local shopkeepers.

"Greenfield School is having a Green Fair soon, and we need your help. Could you please keep us all your newspapers and cardboard boxes?"

"OK," said all the shopkeepers. "If you come and collect them."

Then she went round all the local cafés.

"Greenfield School is having a Green Fair soon, and we need your help. Could you please keep us all your customers' empty cans?"

"Can do," said all the café owners. "If you come and collect them."

Finally, Dani made notices and pinned them up all over town.

GREENFIELD SCHOOL'S GREEN PROJECT

WASTE NOT, WANT NOT

PLEASE HELP BY SAVING
YOUR NEWSPAPERS AND CANS.
TO HAVE THEM COLLECTED PHONE
D. DANIELSON ON 83412.
THANK YOU

"That should get some good results," she said.

It did. The Danielsons' phone never stopped ringing.

"You can come and collect all the old magazines in our attic if you like."

"This is the Top Dog Boarding Kennels. Can you come and collect all our empty dog food cans?" Dani's dad's old car was soon struggling under the weight of all the stuff they collected.

"Where are you going to put it all?"

asked her mum.

"In the garage," said Dani.

The Danielsons carted all the paper and cans into the garage, and soon the garage began to fill up. That left no room for their elderly lawnmower. It had to be moved out into the kitchen. It sat beside the cooker. Dani's mum constantly fell over it.

"Ouch! There goes another pair of new tights. The sooner this project's over the better!"

Then there was no room in the garage for the mountain bikes. They had to be moved out into the hall. They sat right beside the front door. Dani's dad constantly fell over them.

"Ow! Ow! My knee! My poor knee! The sooner this project's over the better!"

In the end, there was no room in

the garage for the Danielsons' old car. It had to be moved out into the street. It sat in front of the house where everything that could fall off it, did. Constantly.

CLANG TING **CLANK** *THUD*.

Mr and Mrs Danielson rubbed their scraped legs and sighed. "We've decided we preferred the frogs and the hedgehogs."

"Cheer up," said Dani. "It won't be long now. Everyone in the class is working really hard. We're sure to win the special prize on Green Fair day."

And everyone *was* working hard on WASTE NOT, WANT NOT. Everyone, that is, but Morris Clump. He was working hard on something else. A special project of his own. He, and brothers Boris and Norris, now had a plan that would ruin all Dani's hard work. And whenever he thought about it, Morris Clump smiled to himself. Horribly.

Chapter Seven

After a while, Dani got quite used to working on the compost heap. She wore her dad's big garden overalls, her mum's rubber gloves, and the nose clips her brothers always wore when they went swimming. Mr Maitland was really pleased with her efforts and brought her an activator and some lime to put on the heap to help the composting get started. Even grumpy Mr Merridew donated an old piece of carpet from his little room to keep the top of the heap from getting too damp. Best of all, Miss Wheeler noticed how well the compost heap was coming along.

"I'm really pleased with the way you've been working on this project, Dani," she said. "You're really making an effort. But remember, no slipping back into your old daring ways."

"No, Miss Wheeler," grinned Dani. "I really think I've got over that."

"That's all you know," muttered Morris Clump, who had been eavesdropping while pretending to tie his shoelaces.

"What a wally," thought Dani, turning round and practically falling over him. "There are no shoelaces on slip-on shoes."

The time for the Green Fair drew near and there was great excitement in Greenfield School. All the classes had been secretly working on their own exhibits for the fair. But some of the secrets had leaked out. Like Primary Four's paper recycling project. They had left their plastic buckets filled with strips of newspaper and water to soak overnight, and Mr Merridew had fallen over them.

TRIP SLOSH **SPLODGE** SQUELCH

SLIIIIIIIIIIIIDE...

"Bloomin' projects!"

And Primary One's bottle band was so secret it could be heard all over the school...

SHISKA SHISKA BOOM BOOM POP POP POP

...while Primary Two's metal snakes, made from threading string through tin cans, could not be kept quiet either.

SLITHER SLITHER RATTLE RATTLE CLANK CLANK CLANK.

Dani's class were making masks out of all the cereal packets they had collected. There were masks of dogs, cats, Batman, clowns, even some painted with bandages and glasses to look like the invisible man. The class intended to wear them on Green Fair day as well as having some for sale. Dani had spent a long time painting very special masks that looked like dragons for Roderick, Jamie and herself.

"No one else will have masks like these," she thought.

Then she caught Morris Clump peering over her shoulder and copying her ideas.

"Copycat," she said. "Why don't you think up ideas of your own?"

But Morris Clump said nothing. He

just smiled. Knowingly.

At last the day of the Green Fair arrived, and Dani's dad ferried Dani and the twins to the school with all the papers and cans from the garage. Dani borrowed Mr Merridew's squeaky old barrow and wheeled her collection into the hall. The hall was piled high with neatly stacked papers and cans. The school really had done well.

"Very well done indeed, Dani," beamed Miss Wheeler when she saw how much Dani had collected. "This is splendid. When we come to sell all this for charity, it should fetch a tidy sum. Now, make your collection into two neat piles."

"Right," said Dani, then left that job to Roderick and Jamie. "I'm just going to fork up my compost heap," she said. "People will be keen to see what can be done with smelly old waste. I've made up some posters saying

THIS WAY TO THE COMPOST HEAP

and I'm going to charge ten pence a time to let people fork it up. It's all in a good cause."

Dani went out into the playground and over to the school wall. Then she stopped and gasped in amazement. Something was wrong. Something was very wrong. Mr Merridew's bricks were there. Mr Merridew's carpet was there. But there was nothing in between them. The compost heap was GONE!

Chapter Eight

"It's just not possible," wailed Dani. "Where can it be? Who would want to steal a compost heap? What use could they possibly make of it? It wasn't even ready yet to be used as compost."

Dani bit her lip. "This could get me into trouble. I bet people will think I've hidden it somewhere as a dare. I'd better search about and see if I can find it before it's too late."

Dani looked all round the school, in the bike sheds, in the old coal cellar, in the dustbins, but the compost heap was nowhere to be found.

"Oh dear," she said, as the crowds began to arrive for the opening of the Green Fair. "Mr Maitland and Miss Wheeler are bound to ask where the compost heap is. What on earth am I going to tell them? Perhaps I'd better hide under my mask while I have a think."

Dani put on her dragon's mask and mingled with the crowds. Soon the fair was in full swing, and everyone seemed to be having a good time. They bought recycled paper

and painted bottle vases,

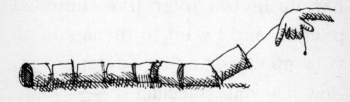

and listened to the metal snakes

and the bottle band.

Then Mr Maitland stood up on the little platform Mr Merridew had erected in the school playground.

"Welcome, everyone, to Greenfield School's Green Fair," he said. "I hope you will find the children's projects and exhibits very interesting. I'm happy to say our local charities will find the contents of this box very interesting too. So far the Green Fair has collected over five hundred pounds, and I want to thank you all very much for being so generous. Now, if anyone is feeling hungry or thirsty, I believe afternoon tea is about to be served in the school dining-room. Miss Wheeler will lead the way."

Miss Wheeler led the way and threw open the dining-hall doors with a flourish. She knew the dining-room looked well. She had set all the tables herself the day before. Then she gave a startled gasp.

"Oh no!" she cried. "Just look at the mess!"

Everyone, including Dani, crowded in at the doors to have a look. And there was a mess. All the tables which had been daintily set out with china cups and saucers were now covered in something else. Something smelly and horrible.

"Oh no," muttered Dani in disbelief. "I've just found my compost heap."

Chapter Nine

"Dani Danielson," yelled Miss Wheeler, catching sight of Dani and grabbing her by the collar. "I know it's you even under your dragon mask. This is all your doing, isn't it? It was a dare, wasn't it? And I thought you had stopped all that. I should have known better. Well, you just come with me, my girl, and we'll find Mr Maitland. He'll deal with you."

"But I didn't...I wasn't...I wouldn't..."

Dani tried to protest.

Just then, Mr Maitland came hurrying up. "Disaster," he cried.

"Disaster is right," said Miss Wheeler. "Dani Danielson's gone too far this time. This time she really is in serious trouble. Do you know what she's done with the compost heap."

"Compost heap? " cried Mr Maitland. "Never mind the compost heap! The cash box with all the money in it for the charities has been stolen. I just stepped down from the platform for a moment to see what all the commotion in the dining-room was about, and when I looked round the cash box was gone."

Then Dani saw it all.

"A diversion," she muttered. "That's what it was. Don't you see? The compost on the tables was a diversion to distract everyone's attention, so that the cash box could be stolen. Did you see anyone nearby?" she asked the head teacher.

"Yes," he said slowly. "Someone in a dragon's mask like yours."

"Morris Clump," said Dani. "He was making masks identical to mine." And she looked over at the school gates. Three dragon-masked figures were sidling towards them.

The Clump Gang!

Dani wriggled out of Miss Wheeler's grasp.

"Stop, thieves!" she yelled, and chased after the Clumps.

The Clump brothers broke into a run and headed out through the school gates.

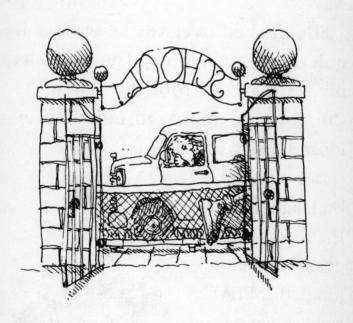

"Oh no!" thought Dani. "If they get over into the farmer's field and into the woods beyond I'll never catch them. I'll never be able to prove they did all this, and I didn't. Perhaps I can head them off if I climb the school wall. They've got to run along that way."

She dashed over to the wall, and quickly scrambled up. The wall was higher than she thought. When the Clump gang appeared below, they looked a long way down.

"Dare I jump," Dani agonised. "Dare I? Oh dear, here goes." And she jumped...SPLAT... right down on top of Morris Clump.

"Ow! No! Help! Gerroff!" he yelled as his dragon mask slipped, and the school cash box fell from his grasp. His two brothers, Boris and Norris, rushed up to help him just as Dani's two brothers rushed up to help her.

"Oh no, you don't," said the twins, sitting on Boris and Norris. "Looks like you lot have got some explaining to do. Lucky we were looking for Dani when we saw what had happened to the compost heap. Lucky we saw her take off after you."

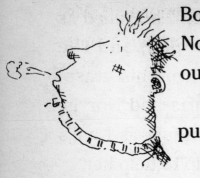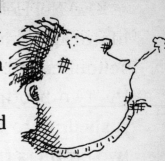

Boris and Norris let out a sigh like a punctured tyre.

Unlucky for them the Danielson twins were big lads.

Later that afternoon, when the Clump gang had been removed to the local police station to help the police with their enquiries, Miss Wheeler apologised to Dani.

"I'm sorry I blamed you, Dani," she said, "but when I saw all that compost on the tea tables I thought you had done it for a dare."

"That's all right, Miss Wheeler," grinned Dani. "I think I really am cured of doing dares, except when I dare myself, and somehow that's different."

The following Monday morning, Mr Maitland had a special announcement to make at Assembly.

"Greenfield School's Green Fair," he said, "was a great success, and I want to thank everyone who took part. I especially want to thank Dani Danielson for her quick thinking and daring which helped recover the stolen cash box, and catch the thieves. I don't think the Clump gang will give us any more trouble for a while. And I'm going to award Dani's class the special prize for all the hard work they and Dani put into the WASTE NOT, WANT NOT project. The special prize is a trip to McCluskey's Circus to see the famous daredevil bareback horse riders."

Everybody cheered and slapped Dani on the back. Then Dot and Ben grinned at each other, nudged Dani and said, "When we're at the circus, dare you to ask Mr McCluskey for some horse manure to start another compost heap."

"OK," Dani grinned back, "but after you. I've thought of a way of not doing dares. I just say,

DARERS DO IT FIRST!"